Folk Tales From Scotland

The Sleeping King

SPHERE BOOKS LIMITED
London and Sydney

Many people said they had seen horsemen riding in the Eildon Hills. When the moon was full, a round, silver plate on black velvet, armoured, mysterious figures jousted and raced in the Hills only to fade into the shadows.

Sometimes a young man would ride out to join them and was never seen again.

The old men said it was the Sleeping King and his knights.

"When Scotland is in danger, they will awake and help us," they said wisely.

"They train in their dreams, and it is only their dreams we see in the moonlight."

Canobie Dick had seen the horsemen many times. Dick was a horse-dealer and he knew more about horses than anyone. He lived with his father and their horses. Dick preferred

horses to people. When he sold a horse, he always made sure that the new owner would treat the animal kindly.

Sometimes he undertook special assignments. Once he was asked to find a horse for the daughter of the laird. He travelled all over Scotland and finally found a gentle, glossy-coated pony. Little Mary was delighted and could soon ride nearly as well as her father.

One night when Dick was riding home he saw a beautiful white stallion just ahead of him. The animal stopped as if waiting for Dick to follow him. Dick called out to the horse but the animal kept just out of reach. Then one moment, the horse stood still at the top of a hill, proudly outlined against the sky and next moment, he had disappeared. Dick searched

until it was dark, but there was no trace of the creature.

Several times Dick saw the horse. His father said it was the King's mount.

"Don't follow him son. You may not be able to find your way home."

Dick laughed. He knew every inch of the hills. But when he next saw the horse, he turned and did not follow.

It was soon after this that the village was raided. The raiders were men of the darkness. The came suddenly and without warning, riding across fields, ruining crops. They took what they wanted, horses, sheep and cattle and left with the dawn.

The raiders became more daring and their behaviour more ruthless and demanding.

Soon the village was ruled by the invaders. Any objection was immediately dealt with. Houses were burnt and crops ruined.

Then one night, they captured the laird's daughter, Mary and held her hostage.

There was despair in the village. They all loved the lass and would not risk her life. The men gathered together.

"There is nothing we can do," said one.

"All my crops are ruined," said another.

"They burnt my house and stole my horse."

"They took my sheep."

"We must fight," said Dick. "We must show them that we are not afraid."

"They will kill the lass," the men objected.

"We must rescue her," said Dick. "We

must find her before they can harm her."

They made their plans carefully. They would lie in ambush for the raiders.

For two nights no one came. On the third night, just as the moon rose, the noise of horses' hoofs thundered in their ears. The raiders had become confident and did not expect any resistance and were taken by surprise.

The villagers fought fiercely but the raiders were stronger and better armed. Once they overcame their initial surprise, the raiders gained ground and pushed the villagers back. Then a burning brand was thrown on to the roof of a house and hungry flames quickly engulfed the building. Soon several houses were ablaze. Dick thought the whole village would be razed

to the ground.

Curiously it seemed to Dick that there were now more men fighting the raiders than there had been at the beginning of the attack. The smoke from the burning houses was so thick that his eyes smarted and he thought he was mistaken. Dick looked more closely at the man fighting next to him. Dick had never seen him before: he was a stranger. He had a magnificent horse and even in this moment of danger, Dick's training as a horse-dealer made him admire the animal.

Looking around, Dick realized that there were several such strangers, each riding equally magnificent beasts and all fighting the raiders.

Dick knew that they were knights and he wondered where they had come from. Each

man wore a mail, knee-length tunic and a helmet. Their round shields warded off the attackers' blows and the knights swung their swords from side to side, driving the raiders back.

Then Dick saw the white stallion. Its rider wore a bright red cloak and was obviously the leader.

Suddenly the fight was over. The raiders fled leaving several buildings smouldering. But Dick knew they would not come back and that Mary must be rescued before it was too late.

He followed the raiders as they fled. Somehow he was not surprised to see the white

stallion ahead of him.

They rode all day until the village was left far behind and all the time they kept the raiders in sight.

As soon as they saw the fortress, the white stallion lengthened its stride. Deliberately its rider showed himself to the raiders. As one man, the raiders turned to follow him. Dick knew the knight was acting as a decoy.

Quickly Dick dismounted. Cautiously he began to search the building. At one end was a door and sitting on the floor, leaning on the door was a guard. Dick was sure Mary was a prisoner behind that door.

Dick jumped with fright when he felt a tap on his shoulder. A knight had come up quietly behind him.

"Leave the guard to me," he said. "You rescue the lassie."

Dick nodded silently and stood to one side to allow the knight to pass by. Quickly he hid in a doorway.

He watched in amazement as the knight walked forward. The knight prodded the guard with his sword.

"Awake rapscallion," the knight said. "I have a matter to sort out with you." He pushed the surprised guard with the tip of his sword disdainfully. "Your tunic sullies my sword, you lilly-livered varmint."

The guard rose slowly to his feet. Upright he was a giant of a man with long arms.

"We will settle this outside, you slow witted cur," the knight again pushed the guard.

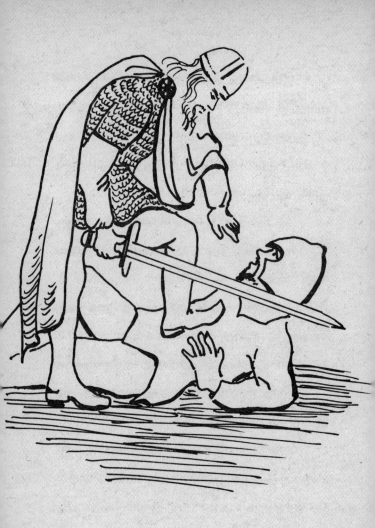

Still dazed with sleep, the guard slowly lumbered to the courtyard with the knight impatiently hurrying him from behind.

"Mount your horse or I will cut off your head now," commanded the knight.

At last the guard came to his senses. Quickly he and the knight mounted their horses. They rode their horses towards each other at full gallop. When they crashed, both men were thrown from their horses by the impact. The guard lay on his back, stunned and unable to move. The tip of the knight's sword found the soft flesh at the base of the guard's throat. He rested his right foot on the man's chest.

"Get up and fight, you cowardly dog," said the knight.

Awkwardly, the man clambered to his feet.

The guard was taller than the knight, but large and cumbersome, and slow on his feet. He swung his sword from side to side and Dick feared that one blow would fell the knight. He need not have worried. The knight was well trained and faster and the guard was no match for him.

While the two men fought, Dick made his way to the now unguarded door. It was locked but gave way when he pushed it with his shoulder.

In the dim light from the open doorway, Dick could see a small, dark, windowless room. Mary lay on a pile of rags in the far corner. Her captors had not fed her and she was too weak to walk. Dick carried her to his horse.

As they rode away, Dick heard the knight gallop across the field. For a moment the knight

raised his arm in salute and then he was hidden by the trees of a nearby wood.

Dick knew his horse was tired and must be rested. He also knew that Mary had suffered during her captivity and needed to rest.

When Dick thought they were safe from pursuit, he found shelter for them in a cave. Nearby was a small stream. Mary drank thirstily.

"We will rest for a while," said Dick.

Soon Mary was asleep. Dick kept watch. His job would not be finished until he had delivered Mary back to her father.

As the sun's first rays stole across the sky, Dick gently roused Mary. He helped her on to the horse and they set off once more.

It was mid morning when they reached the village. A look-out spotted them and the church bell

was rung.

At last Dick could give in to his fatigue. It seemed as if the church bells pealed inside his head, louder and louder. Willing hands helped him to his house.

Dick could not understand why no one said anything about the knights. It seemed that no one had seen them and Dick began to wonder if he had imagined them. There had been so much smoke and fighting he was no longer clear about the events of that night.

Then one evening, Dick saw the white stallion again. Dick followed the horse but he could not catch up with it. The horse led him to the brow of a hill and disappeared. He was determined to find out where the horse had gone and he searched until dark. But there was no trace of the animal.

Dick often visited distant farms to buy horses. One evening he started for home much later than usual. The farmer's wife suggested that he stay the night.

"There's going to be a storm," she said. "You are welcome to stay in the barn tonight. You'll be safe and dry there and we've plenty of food for supper."

Dick thanked her but said that he would rather make for home.

It had been a very hot day and the evening was still as it often is before a storm.

At first there was just a gentle breeze which ruffled Dick's hair. Gradually it became stronger until the young saplings bent and Dick had to fight against it. The blue cloudless sky darkened, lightning flashed and thunder rumbled uneasily in the hills.

Then the rain came and within minutes Dick was soaked to the skin.

He wished that he had stayed at the farm but he could not find his way back. Dick wondered aimlessly until he was lost. Then from the darkness ahead came the sound of horse's hoofs. It was the white stallion. Dick followed the animal and to his relief, the horse led him to a small wooden hut. As Dick found the hut, the white stallion galloped away.

Thankfully Dick stumbled inside. Soon he had a fire lit and had dried out his clothes. He rubbed his horse down.

"I'm sorry I haven't any food for you," he said patting the horse.

Then Dick slept. He didn't wake until morning and when he looked out he found that the valley

through which he had ridden was flooded. The white stallion had saved his life.

Quickly Dick made his way home. There was to be a fair in the village and he hoped to sell all his horses.

By mid-morning the village square was full of people. Stands had been set up and they were loaded with all kinds of merchandise. There were spices and perfumes from distant foreign lands, pewter tankards and copper pans for cooking, ribbons and muslins, silks and satins. There was butter and cheese, milk and ham. There were chickens and goats, sheep and cattle. Dick led his horses to a fenced-off area on one side of the square.

Business was brisk and the stands emptied and coins clinked. By late afternoon, Dick had just two

horses left.

He felt very tired as he rode home, taking the two unsold horses with him. Outside the village, he was stopped by a tall man. The man's clothes were old and creased, as if, Dick thought, he had been sleeping in them.

"Good day, sir," said the stranger. " Are those horses for sale?" He pointed at the two horses Dick was leading.

Dick nodded. The man offered Dick two gold pieces but Dick said that the price was not high enough.

"They are fine horses," he said. "Strong and young."

The man agreed. "I will meet you here tomorrow and we shall agree a price."

Dick hurried on. He wondered where the man

had come from and why he wore such old, curious clothes.

Dick met the stranger several times before a price was agreed.

"You strike a hard bargain," said the man.

Dick looked at the gold coins the man had given him. They were very old.

"I have never been paid with coins like these," said Dick.

"They are very valuable, " said the stranger. "It is my custom," the stranger went on, "to seal a deal like this with a drink. Will you come to my place?"

Dick agreed.

"You must not be frightened or alarmed at anything you see. Providing you show no fear, no harm will come to you."

Puzzled Dick followed the man. They rode for

a long time and at last they came to a hummock called the Lucken Hare. The stranger led the way to a concealed door. Dick thought that he would never be able to find the door alone.

The stranger opened the door and Dick found himself in a huge cavern. Around the cavern were sleeping knights in their armour. Nearby were their sleeping horses.

Dick recognised the nights as the men who had helped to fight off the raiders at the village. A little apart from the knights, on a white couch lay the knights' leader. At his feet, was the white stallion Dick had seen so many times.

"I've seen these men before," exclaimed Dick.

The stranger said nothing. He pointed to an enormous round table. On it was a sword and a horn.

"You have the choice," said the stranger, "of blowing the horn or drawing the sword. Whoever makes the correct choice will be King of all Britain."

Dick looked at the man in bewilderment. "I don't understand," he said.

The stranger looked at him impatiently. "You should either blow the horn or draw the sword."

Dick did not understand but he felt he had better do as the man suggested. With trembling hands he lifted the horn to his lips and blew.

Immediately Dick knew that he made made the wrong choice. A huge blast of cold air swept through the cavern. Dick struggled to keep his feet on the ground but it was no use. His feet were swept from under him and he was carried by the wind out of the cave.

Dick found himself wandering about an unfamiliar hillside. He was lost and exhausted when he fell asleep.

The next day, a shepherd came to the house of Dick's father. He explained that that morning when he had been looking for a lost lamb, he had found Dick fast asleep. It had been difficult to wake him and when he did so, Dick looked at him with frightened eyes.

"He told me," said the shepherd, "that he had been taken to a cavern. There he had seen several knights and their horses." The man paused doubtfully. "He said they were all fast asleep!"

"Where is my son?" asked Dick's father anxiously.

"I tried to make him come home,"

answered the shepherd. "But he wouldn't. He kept on saying that he must find the cavern and withdraw the sword."

"What sword?" asked Dick's father.

"I don't know. Your son said that there was a horn and a sword. He had blown the horn in error and he wanted to withdraw the sword instead." The shephered hesitated. "He said that if he could find the cavern and withdraw the sword he would be King of all Britain."

Dick's father was very concerned. His son had mentioned knights before.

"I fear," he said, "that the damp air has given my son the ague. His mind is affected. Please take me to where you last saw him and I will find him."

The shepherd led Dick's father to the spot

on the hillside where he had found the lad. Dick's father searched the hills for three days and three nights but he could find no trace of his son.

Then, as he was about to return home, he stumbled and there at his feet was a large horn. He picked it up. It was very heavy and encrusted with jewels. He blew the horn, hoping his son would hear. But there was no response.

Sometimes today, when an adventurous traveller looses his bearings in the hills, he will tell how the sound of a horn guided him to safety.

Illustrated by John Fane

© C.E.S.
First Published 1979
Published in this edition by Sphere Books Ltd 1985
30–32 Gray's Inn Road, London WC1X 8JL

Printed and bound in Great Britain by
Cox & Wyman Ltd, Reading